For Stephen – can't think of my childhood
without thinking of you

A.

To Hannah and Max McFeely

L.T.

First American Edition 2013
Kane Miller, A Division of EDC Publishing

Text © 2013 Atinuke
Illustrations © 2013 Lauren Tobia

Published by arrangement with Walker Books Ltd
87 Vauxhall Walk, London SE11 5HJ

Kane Miller, A Division of EDC Publishing
P.O. Box 470663
Tulsa, OK 74147-0663
www.kanemiller.com
www.edcpub.com

Library of Congress Control Number: 2012954083

Printed in Guangdong, China
1 2 3 4 5 6 7 8 9 10
ISBN: 978-1-61067-173-6

SPLASH, ANNA HIBISCUS!

ATINUKE ✿ LAUREN TOBIA

Kane Miller
A DIVISION OF EDC PUBLISHING

Anna Hibiscus lives in Africa.
Amazing Africa.

Anna Hibiscus is at the beach
with her whole family.
The sun is hot. The sand is hot.
The laughing waves are splashing.

Anna Hibiscus looks at the splashing waves.

Grandmother and Grandfather
are reading their newspapers.

Papa and Uncle Tunde
are talking to the fishermen.

Mama and the aunties
are braiding their hair.

The cousins are busy too.

Joy, Clarity and Common Sense
are on their phones.

Benz and Wonderful
are playing soccer
with the beach boys.

Chocolate is burying
Angel in the sand.

"Angel!" shouts Anna Hibiscus.
"Come and splash with me!"
"I can't," says Angel. "I'm almost buried."

"Chocolate!" shouts Anna Hibiscus.
"Come and splash!"
"No," says Chocolate.
"You come and help me dig!"

But Anna Hibiscus does not
want to dig in the hot sand.
She wants to splash
in the laughing waves.
And she wants to splash
with somebody!

"Benz! Wonderful!"
shouts Anna Hibiscus.
"Come and splash with me!"

Benz and Wonderful are running
too fast to hear Anna Hibiscus.

"Kick the ball!" shouts Benz.
"Wondaful girl, kick'am!"
shouts Wonderful.

But Anna Hibiscus does not want
to kick balls on the hot sand.
She wants to splash
in the laughing waves.
And she wants to splash
with somebody!

"Joy! Clarity! Common Sense!
Will you come and play in the waves with me?"
asks Anna Hibiscus.

"No, no!" laughs Joy.
"We are too big now for playing," says Clarity.
"And we are too busy," says Common Sense.

Anna Hibiscus stamps away.
She wants to splash in the laughing waves.
And she wants to splash with somebody!

"Mama?" Anna Hibiscus asks her mother.

"First I need to finish braiding,"
   says Anna's mother.
"And after that it will be time to eat."

   Anna Hibiscus kicks the sand.

"Go away to kick your sand,"
   says Auntie Joli.

"You will spoil the corn,"
   says Auntie Grace.

"Papa?" asks Anna Hibiscus.

"Don't interrupt," says Anna's father.
"Wait until I have finished talking."

Anna Hibiscus waits a long time.
But the men don't ever stop talking.

Anna Hibiscus looks at Grandmother
and Grandfather.
From underneath the newspapers
she can hear snoring.
Anna Hibiscus whispers,
"Grandmother? Grandfather?"
But there is no answer.

Anna Hibiscus looks around.
There is nobody left to ask.

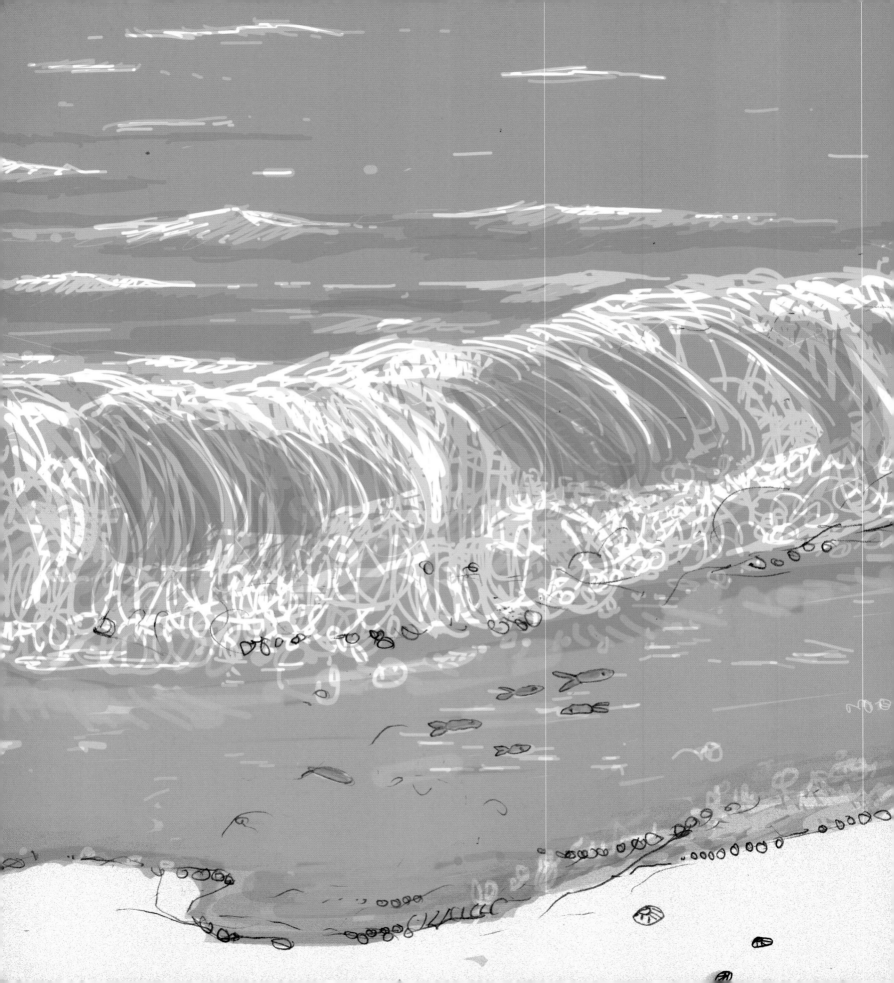

There are only the waves jumping and splashing.
They want to splash with somebody.

Splash!

The white waves splash
Anna Hibiscus.
Oh! Anna Hibiscus
splashes back.

Jump!

The white waves jump on
Anna Hibiscus.
Oh! Anna Hibiscus
jumps back.

Hee-hee!

The white waves laugh at Anna Hibiscus.
Oh! Anna Hibiscus laughs back.
"Hee-hee!
Hee-hee! Hee-hee!"

Hee-hee! Hee-hee! Hee-hee!

Chocolate hears Anna laughing.
She stops digging.
Angel shouts to Chocolate,
"Wait for me!"

Benz and Wonderful hear Anna laughing.
"Look! Let's go!" shouts Benz.
"Wondaful!" shouts Wonderful.

Hee-hee! Hee-hee! Hee-hee! Hee-hee! Hee-hee! Hee-hee! Hee-hee! Hee-hee!

Joy, Clarity and Common Sense hear Anna laughing.

"We are not that old," says Clarity.

"We're not that busy," says Common Sense.

"Phones are so boring," says Joy. "Come on!"

Hee-hee! Hee-hee! Hee-hee!

Anna's mother and the aunties
hear Anna laughing.
"I'm hot!" says Anna's mother.
"Let's eat later," says
Auntie Joli.

Anna's father stops talking
when he hears Anna laughing.
"O-ya!" shouts Uncle Tunde.
"I'm coming!" shouts
Anna's father.

Anna's laughing is so loud
that Grandmother and Grandfather wake up.
"What are we waiting for?"
says Grandmother.
"Let's go!" says Grandfather.

Hee-hee! Hee-hee! Hee-hee! Hee-hee! Hee-hee! Hee-hee! Hee-hee!

Anna Hibiscus looks around.
She sees Chocolate and Angel
    and Benz and Wonderful and Clarity
        and Joy and Common Sense,
            and her mother and the aunties,

and her father
and Uncle Tunde,
    and even Grandmother
            and Grandfather
all running down the hot yellow sand to –

SPLASH!

in the laughing waves.

"Hee-hee!"
laughs Anna Hibiscus.

"Hee-hee!"
laughs the whole entire family.
"Hee-hee!" laugh the splashing waves.

Anna Hibiscus lives in Africa.
Amazing Africa.
Anna Hibiscus is amazing too.